E
Mor

Mora, Pat.
The night the moon
fell : a Maya myth

MAR 0 3			
MAR 1 8			

Demco, Inc. 38-293

The Night the Moon Fell

For Elizabeth Mills who journeys within
P M

Text copyright © 2000 by Pat Mora
Illustrations copyright © 2000 by Domi

Groundwood Books/Douglas & McIntyre
720 Bathurst Street, Suite 500, Toronto, Ontario M5S 2R4

Distributed in the USA by Publishers Group West
1700 Fourth Street, Berkeley, CA 94710

Canadian Cataloguing in Publication Data
Mora, Pat
The night the moon fell
"A Groundwood book."
ISBN 0-88899-398-6
1. Moon — Mythology — Juvenile literature. 2. Mayas — Folklore.
3. Maya mythology — Juvenile literature. I. Domi. II. Title.
PZ8.1.M668Ni 2000   j398.2'089'974152   C99-932951-0

Printed and bound in China by Everbest Printing Co. Ltd.

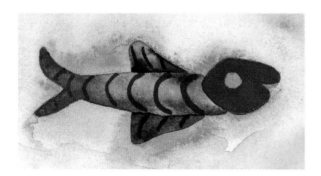

Pat Mora has taken the traditional Mopan Maya (Belize) myth, in which the moon is a young weaver and the Milky Way a fish, found in *The Mysterious Maya* by George E. Stuart and Gene S. Stuart (National Geographic), and originally told by Eric Thompson, and transformed it to show a moon who finds a way to save herself, making the archetypal journey from homeland to a strange new world and back again.

The Night the Moon Fell

A MAYA MYTH RETOLD BY

Pat Mora

ILLUSTRATED BY

Domi

A Groundwood Book Douglas & McIntyre Toronto Vancouver Buffalo

One night long ago, Luna the moon hummed high in the night sky. Stars twinkled, and Luna's friend the wind dozed nearby. The night was hushed and peaceful.

Suddenly, the sky shook. A loud *WHOOSH!* rattled the stars and startled the moon. Luna's grandfather had shot his blowgun, and Luna jumped in surprise. She lost her balance and started to roll and roll.

Luna rolled through stars, and she rolled through clouds. She rolled, rolled down to the earth and splashed into the ocean's cold, dark waves. She broke into shimmering slivers and bits on the sandy bottom of the sea.

The huge sky became black and still as the deepest ocean. Stars shut their eyes. Flowers bowed their heads, and all the birds in the world rose looking for the moon. They flew into loud storms. They soared down black canyons. They darted into huge caves calling,

> "Luna, come back, bring us your light.
> Shine your white light for us tonight."

Silence.

Luna's amigo, the wind, raced up mountains whispering and then roaring,

> "Luna, come back, bring us your light.
> Shine your white light for us tonight."

All the world waited. All the world listened.
Silence.
Where was the moon?

The tiny fish at the bottom of the sea knew. They saw Luna's white glow, and they heard her lonely song.

> "Where am I? Where's the sky?
> Broken, sad, lost am I."

The fish swam round and around the broken moon. "What can we do? What can we do?" they whispered.

"We'll be your friends," said the tiniest fish. "What's your name?"

"Luna," the moon sniffled.

"Are you the shining light that hums high in the sky?" asked the roundest fish.

Luna sniffed,

> "I was the light high in the sky,
> Now broken, sad, lost am I."

The tiny fish and Luna looked up together. They looked up through all that deep, dark water. The little fish missed seeing the moonlight high in the night sky. They missed playing in Luna's white light.